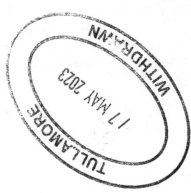

To Dad and Tanya

Special thanks to Benjamin Scott

Bloomsbury Publishing, London, Berlin, New York and Sydney

First published in Great Britain in February 2012 by Bloomsbury Publishing Plc
50 Bedford Square, London, WC1B 3DP

A CIP catalogue record for this book is available from the British Library

ISBN 978 1 4088 1579 3

Typeset by Hewer Text UK Ltd, Edinburgh
Printed in Great Britain by Clays Ltd, St Ives Plc, Bungay, Suffolk

1 3 5 7 9 10 8 6 4 2

www.bloomsbury.com
www.starfighterbooks.com

MAX CHASE

BLOOMSBURY

LONDON BERLIN NEW YORK SYDNEY

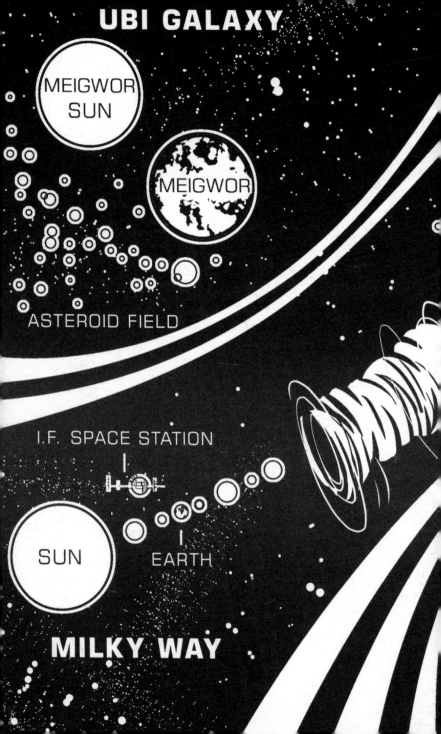

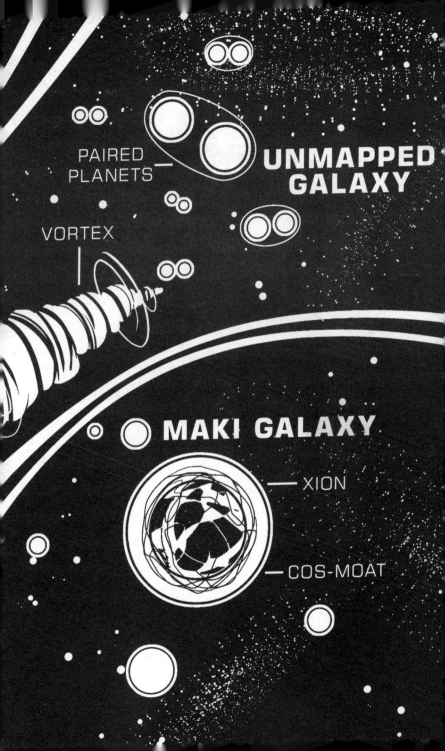

STAR FIGHTERS

An elite fighting team sworn to protect and defend the galaxy

It is the year 5012 and the Milky Way galaxy is under attack . . .

After the Universal War . . . a war that almost brought about the destruction of every known universe . . . the planets in the Milky Way banded together to create the Intergalactic Force – an elite fighting team sworn to protect and defend the galaxy.

Only the brightest and most promising students are accepted into the Intergalactic Force Academy, and only the very best cadets reach the highest of their ranks and become . . .

To be a Star Fighter is to dedicate your life to one mission: *Peace in Space*. They are given the coolest weapons, the fastest spaceships – and the most dangerous missions. Everyone at the Intergalactic Force Academy wants to be a Star Fighter someday.

Do YOU have what it takes?

Chapter 1

'You are astro-bug-stupid!' Diesel yelled. His yellow eyes flashed and the band of hair that stretched across his head flamed crimson. 'There's no way DeathRays can work inside a nebular cloud.'

'Take me to a nebular!' Otto's voice boomed through the two lumps on either side of his neck. 'And I'll show you!' The Meigwor bounty hunter's voice was unnaturally loud, as if he was always shouting.

Peri tried to ignore their argument, which

had started the moment they left the Meigwor battleship. He focused on the image filling the *Phoenix*'s 360-monitor. According to the ship's computer, their destination, the high-tech mining planet of Xion, was less than one million miles away.

'*Phoenix*, magnify image,' he said.

The giant pulsing orange-and-blue orb expanded to fill the screen. Xion was surrounded by a gigantic space highway. Over twelve-hundred lanes of silver-and-purple Astrophalt twisted and slithered round the planet like a tangle of space-snakes.

Peri flexed his fingers. The *Phoenix*'s floating control panel slid closer as if it knew what he wanted. It felt like he'd been flying the ship all his life. Yesterday he had been just an average first-year Intergalactic Force Academy cadet, lucky to be selected for even a simple training mission. Now he

was on a mission to rescue a kidnapped prince. But the biggest shock was he had found out that he was part-bionic, modified by his parents to operate the *Phoenix*.

He activated his most recent discovery, *The Space Spotter's Guide*. Instantly, over a dozen arrows appeared on the 360-monitor, pointing to different dangers. Peri scrolled past the micro-mines then hovered over the space-pods guarding the entrance to the space highway and clicked. An InfoBox popped up on his screen:

Xion Toll-Takers, third class

DESCRIPTION: Flying tollbooths, guarding entrance to Xion space highway.

HAZARDS: X-cite lasers, ship-deep scanners, cloaking detectors.

WARNING: 'Strictly no Meigwors.'

'They're going to *love* Otto as much as we do,' Peri muttered. 'We need a way round all that security.'

Peri tapped the monitor and zoomed out. The entire space-highway system was surrounded by a giant dark blue bubble. *The Space Spotter's Guide* flashed another warning:

Cos-Moats

DESCRIPTION: Thicker than rock-eating slime. More corrosive than sun-worm snot. Standard shield useless.

HAZARDS: Acidic ooze.

RECOMMENDATION: Avoid.

'Now what?' Peri asked himself, wishing Selene was with them. She had been sneaking on to the *Phoenix* for years and had stowed away when Peri and Diesel were launched into space. She would have known how to activate the *Phoenix*'s anti-moat shields. But she was stuck on Meigwor as insurance that Peri and Diesel would complete their 'mission'.

'Don't touch me!' Otto screeched.

Thud! Peri spun round to see Diesel sprawled on the floor. The half-Martian bounced back up. His yellow eyes flashed as he assumed the cosmic-combat position. But even with his hair standing on end, Diesel barely reached the ammo-belts criss-crossing Otto's chest.

'Wastoid,' Diesel shouted. 'I'm the best cadet gunner in the history of the Intergalatic Force. I can reassemble a blaster in ten galactic seconds.'

The two lumps protruding from Otto's freakishly long neck throbbed with anger as he yelled, 'I can reassemble it with one hand, and squash you with the other!'

Peri sighed. They didn't have time for this. He turned the ship's internal-com volume to maximum and blasted through the speakers, 'Stick an asteroid in it, both of you!'

Diesel and Otto turned to face Peri. Their arguing stopped.

'Why didn't you tell me we'd reached Xion?!' demanded Otto, using his massive body to force Peri from the control panel.

'Because you were too busy fighting,' Peri said, pushing back.

'To the planet surface, now!' Otto ordered.

Diesel elbowed between Otto and Peri. 'Who died and made you supreme commander? I'm the oldest cadet on this ship and ranked top in my class on leadership qualities and I —'

Otto interrupted, 'Don't you want revenge on the Xions for attacking your galaxy?! I know what I'm doing.'

Peri snapped his fingers and the control panel flew across to him. 'How do we cross the Cos-Moat?' Peri yelled to be heard over Otto and Diesel.

'Just blast your way through it!' Otto tutted. 'Do I have to tell you everything?!'

'What about,' Diesel paused, running a hand through his now purple hair, 'if we use the *Phoenix's* pulsar-cannon belt?'

'No, you cosmic dope!' Otto snapped. 'Pulsar-cannons are totally unstable weapons! You'll blow us up too! Don't you have any nuclear devices?! They're much safer!'

Peri raised his hands to silence them. 'Isn't this an undercover mission? Don't we need the element of surprise to rescue the prince? Maybe we should find the thinnest section of moat – then our shields will stand a chance of surviving the acidic ooze.'

Otto stared at Peri without blinking his beady eyes. 'That's what I said! Blast us through the thinnest section of moat! That's an order!'

Peri clenched his fist – the sooner this mission was over the better. He activated a photonic sweep of the moat and set a course for the thinnest stretch of sludge. As the ship neared, the dark blue liquid sparkled as if it was reflecting sunlight. But it shouldn't have. It was on the dark side of the planet. 'The Cos-Moat is electrified!' Peri exclaimed. 'We'll be fried.'

'If the space-sharks don't get us first,' Diesel added.

'You don't *really* believe in space-sharks,

do you?!' The Meigwor's lipless mouth twitched into what could have been a smile. 'I forget. Inferior species still believe in these myths.'

Duurrr-iiiig! An alarm sounded and a com-screen whirled up from the middle of the control panel. Selene's face flickered as the monitor came to life.

'Hello, Peri and Diesel,' Selene said. 'I am being treated well . . . by our Meigwor friends . . .' Selene sounded like a robot.

It's like she's reading from a script, Peri thought.

'Selene, are you OK?' Diesel asked.

Before she could reply, the crimson face of the Meigwor General Rouwgim pushed her aside. 'Otto — give mission report now,' he demanded.

Otto smacked his hands together over his head in salute. 'We have reached Xion, General! I was just briefing the Milky Way monkeys about my cunning plan to rescue the prince . . .'

The screen went dead, whirring back into the control panel.

'You!' Otto boomed, pointing a finger at Peri. 'You cut the general off on purpose!'

'It wasn't me,' Peri replied, checking the controls. 'The Xions are jamming all signals around the planet.'

'Cloak the ship before they notice us!' Otto ordered. 'Full-speed through the Cos-Moat!'

'It's not that easy, Otto,' Peri said as he steered the *Phoenix* closer. 'If we're to stand a chance, we need to find the Cos-Moat's thinnest and most vulnerable spot.'

To the right of them, a small blade-class ship was racing towards the rippling blue moat. His chest filled with hope – it was the type of ship preferred by smugglers. And if they knew a way into Xion, then Peri could follow them. He steered the *Phoenix* into the smugglers' slipstream, tucking in as close as he dared. Jets of sticky sludge arched from the moat like monstrous tentacles and latched on to the smugglers' ship. In the blink of an eye, the small ship was gone, sucked down into the gooey Cos-Moat.

Buuuurrrrppppp! A giant bubble erupted from the moat and popped, spraying the outside of the *Phoenix*. The goo hissed and smoked as it ate through the ship's outer shell.

A frenzy of warning lights lit up the control panel.

'The moat's shorted the cloaking device,' Peri shouted.

'Get out of here!' boomed Otto, his scarlet skin paling to pink. 'Th-th-that moat just ate a ship.'

Peri lunged for the controls. He tried to pull the levers to maximum thrust, but it was as though they were covered in toffee. He hit the emergency boosters. The *Phoenix* still struggled to pull away. The moat was tugging harder, dragging the ship back.

'Peri . . .' Otto's voice was nervous.

'Not now, Otto!' Peri cried, still struggling with the levers.

Eee-ra, eee-ra! Sirens erupted around the Bridge.

'*Peri!*'

Something in Otto's voice made Peri tear his eyes away from the controls. The alien bounty hunter was pointing at the only part of the monitor that was not covered in gloop.

Fear filled Peri's chest like liquid fire.

'Space-sharks!'

Chapter 2

Eight huge space-sharks surged towards the spaceship. They had giant grey shark-heads and beady black eyes. Instead of tails, a pulsing mass of tentacles powered them on, flicking Cos-Moat slime behind them. The sharks opened their hideous mouths, showing rows of jagged purple teeth. Bits of the smugglers' ship were caught between them.

Thuuuddd. Sccrrraatcch. The sharks' teeth gnashed at the *Phoenix*'s hull.

'I told you they were real!' Diesel shouted as Otto hid behind his chair.

Crrraaack! Huge cracks were appearing across the 360-monitor. The *Phoenix*'s shell had been damaged. Peri's Expedition Wear flamed red as a cold sweat made him shiver.

If the monitor shatters, thought Peri, *we're shark bait!*

'What's that smell?' Diesel cried.

Peri sniffed, looking around. 'Oh no . . .' The Cos-Moat had pulled the *Phoenix* to its electrified surface and its blue goo was oozing through the cracks into the Bridge. It stank worse than uranium-toe jam and cosmic-liver ice cream combined. As the goo mixed with the ship's atmosphere, it erupted into sparks as bright as stars.

'We need shields,' Peri shouted, but before he could reach the control panel a hood sprang from his collar and encased his head in a transparent, armoured bubble. *Click.* It sealed him from the air in the ship.

Whoorrrl. The protective helmet's filtration system started.

Peri and Diesel were both sealed in their Expedition Wear, but Otto had dropped to his knees and was gasping for air. Despite the countless blaster-holsters, grenades and survival packs strapped to his body, he had nothing to protect him against the smoke and gas filling the Bridge. The Meigwor's eyes bulged out of the black patches on his crimson face.

'Hang on,' Peri shouted over another *twaaack-craaack.* A space-shark was trying to gnaw its way through the 360-monitor. Every gnash of its teeth was showering the Bridge with white-hot sparks. Peri's hands danced across the control panel. 'Now the shields aren't working.'

'We've got to blast the sharks, or we'll get sucked into the moat,' Diesel yelled.

'We've got to use the *Phoenix*'s pulsar-cannon belt.'

'Isn't it dangerous?' Peri asked.

'You know what they say,' Diesel said, a twinkle in his yellow eyes, '"you can't hunt Venusian crabs without losing a toe".'

THWACK. Two space-sharks hammered against the craft. Peri knew they had to do something.

'Go for it,' he yelled.

As Diesel pulled a lever on the gunnery station, massive spike-like cannons shot out from the side of the ship. The sharks peeled away from the hull, but not far enough.

Peri realised the sharks had to be further away for the cannons to target them. He had to scare them off. Diesel was halfway around the Bridge when Peri slid into the captain's chair. The floating astro-harness snaked around him.

'I hope this works,' he muttered.

Peri shouted, 'Hold on. It's time to play spaceball!'

He nudged the ship into the middle of the swarm of space-sharks, then jammed the Nav-wheel hard, spinning the *Phoenix* in a tight circle. He slammed on the steering thrusters, blasting more power into his manoeuvre. The ship twisted violently like a vortex, throwing everything that was not tied down into the air. Peri had to fight against the G-forces. His astro-harness tightened, crushing him against the chair.

Thud. 'Oooof!' Otto crashed into Peri's chair, tossed by the spinning ship.

Smaaack! The metal cannons punched the sharks in their ugly, slimy mouths. Peri nudged forward again. *Smaack!* The sharks swam further away.

'Yes!' Peri cried.

An angry Diesel sailed by.

'*Mars'rakk!*' the gunner shouted.

'Sorry!' Peri jammed on the brakes, wrestling the *Phoenix* to a standstill.

Diesel lunged for the gunner's chair. Cracking his knuckles, he yelled, 'Eight shark soups, Martian-style, coming up!'

He twisted a zip-dial. Bolts of fiery-green electricity burst from the ship straight for the sharks.

KAA-BLAM!

The sharks exploded, their entrails spewing across the ship's hull. The 360-monitor was splattered with dark blue goo, white shark flesh and bloody lumps.

'Space-shell repair activated,' said the measured voice of the *Phoenix*.

The monitor fizzed as a megawatt charge surged through the outside of the vessel. The dark gloop evaporated to reveal that all the cracks had fused together and the ship was back to normal.

'All systems zip-zapped and moon-shaped.' Peri grinned as the hood on his jacket retracted. The air was breathable again. 'One pest-free Cos-Moat ready to cross.'

Otto staggered to his feet. He looked a little battered, but was still breathing. He pointed a shaky finger over Peri's shoulder.

Peri turned and instantly wished that the

360-monitor wasn't crystal clear again. He would rather not see what he was seeing. An enormous pale white tail swishing back and forth. A gigantic mouth with teeth the size of the smugglers' ship.

Diesel rubbed his eyes as if he could make it go away. 'Is that . . . ?'

The enormous mother of all space-sharks was heading right for them.

Chapter 3

'That thing could eat the *Phoenix* whole!' Diesel cried, as he fired all the pulsar-cannons into the great white space-shark's open mouth. The creature swallowed the shells like Martian mints. '*Klûu'aah*,' Diesel gasped in disbelief as the shark's sides bulged when the shells exploded inside it.

Phuuurrrp! A cloud of smoke appeared behind the shark.

'This space-shark farts our best weapon,' Diesel muttered. 'How do we kill this thing?'

'Blast it again!' Otto wailed, beating his chair.

The shark whipped its tail, driving it on to the *Phoenix*, then it swam away revving up for another attack. Peri knew shooting it wouldn't help. They had to outsmart it.

'I've got a better idea.' Peri gripped the Nav-wheel and fired all thrusters. The *Phoenix* roared forward on a collision course with the shark.

'Are you crazy?!' Otto shouted, trying to wrestle Peri from the captain's chair. 'This isn't a suicide mission.'

'Back off, dumboid,' Diesel said, pulling Otto off Peri. 'Peri may be crazy – but he's not stupid.'

Peri held the ship steady. They whipped past the shark's open mouth and collided with its tail. It was perfect timing. The impact catapulted the *Phoenix* at the

Cos-Moat. Peri flicked on the shields as the ship smacked into the dark blue sludge. The thrusters died in seconds, but it didn't matter. The force of the shark's tail propelled the *Phoenix* out through the other side fast enough to avoid any damage from the acidic ooze.

Peri punched the air.

Diesel grinned at Otto. 'See? Crazy and brilliant.'

A sudden burst of brilliant light blinded Peri. 'What the . . . ?' he said as he shielded his eyes. Peri tried squinting at the source of the light, but only when the *Phoenix* tinted the 360-monitor could he see outside. Two Xion fighter jets had shooting-star-sized searchlights trained on the Bridge of their spaceship.

'Attention. Receiving message from alien ships,' stated the calm voice of the *Phoenix*.

'*Zark, Sakar, Zarak,*' came over the intercom. The alien spoke in a short, clipped language with a strange nasal growl, as if it had a cold.

Peri pressed the bulge under his chin to adjust his SpeakEasy computer chip. All cadets and Star Fighters had the device implanted so they could understand any alien they encountered. His skull crackled with static until he found the right wavelength.

'Diesel, set your language controls to frequency 08.12.77.'

Diesel nodded and they glanced at each other as they heard the message in English for the first time. 'Entering Xion space without permission is an act of war. This is your only warning. Follow us to the tollbooth or be vaporised.'

'Any idea how we deal with the

Toll-Takers?' Peri asked as he followed the Xion fighter jets.

Otto licked the sweat from his neck with his long tongue. 'It doesn't matter! When they find me on board, we'll be obliterated before you can say, "Death to Xion"!'

Peri frowned. He wondered why the Xions and Meigwors hated each other so much. 'Otto, you'd better hide.'

'Cowards hide!' Otto snapped. 'Warriors lie in wait!'

'Well, go *lie in wait*, then,' Peri said.

Otto skulked out of the Bridge.

'What a lamizoid!' Diesel said as he sat down next to Peri. Almost instantly, he sprang out of the chair again. 'Yuck! Meigwor sweat!' He wiped his hand against his trousers. 'The sooner we get him off our ship the better. Look,' he said, twisting around to show Peri the smoking holes in his Expedition-Wear trousers.

'Get your trousers out of my face,' Peri said. 'I need to concentrate.'

The Xion fighter jets guided them to the space highway's only ramp. A new message flashed on the monitor. 'Join the queue, or be disintegrated.'

Its bluntness made Peri realise how unfriendly the Xions were, but he already knew that. They hadn't given the IF Space Station a warning before they blew it to smithereens! His hands gripped the Nav-wheel tighter. He was going to stop these bullies if it was the last thing he ever did.

But, for now, he had a mission to complete.

Peri parked the *Phoenix* behind a ship surrounded by huge translucent sheets of solar-cloth. It looked like a floating angel.

'It's beautiful,' whispered Peri.

Suddenly, the angel's wings unfurled like old-fashioned sails. The ship slid gracefully forward. A thick purple beam of light blazed from the Toll-Taker as it scanned every micro-particle of the craft.

An electric jolt of fear passed through Peri. 'Diesel, what do we do if they find Otto with the scan?'

'I guess we could say he's a stowaway and hand him over,' Diesel replied. 'Only a cosmic wastoid couldn't notice something that big, ugly, hot and sweaty.'

'That's it!' Peri exclaimed, his mind tingling with excitement. 'He's hot and sweaty. They're scanning for heat signatures. If the *Phoenix* is cold enough, it'll hide Otto's body heat.'

'Oh, sure, freeze us to death to save our Meigwor tour guide,' Diesel scoffed.

Peri spun the thermo-dial to cool the ship and an icy blast of air surrounded them. But their teeth barely had time to chatter before their Expedition Wear turned red and started to warm them up.

'You see, not a problem,' Peri started. 'I love this ship.'

The vessel ahead of them entered the space-highway ramp and the *Phoenix* glided to a stop behind a barricade of pulsing red light. An announcement from the Toll-Taker

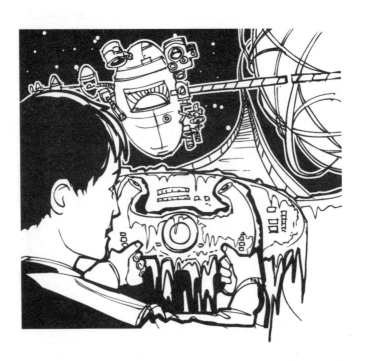

interrupted him: 'Prepare to be inspected. Approach slowly.'

The Nav-wheel was slippery with ice, but Peri guided the *Phoenix* towards the striped guard pod with expert skill.

Durrr-ing! The com-screen rose from the console and flashed into life. A Xion appeared. He wore a bright blue uniform, braided with pink, and a scarlet cap.

'This is Toll-Taker Xerallon.' A beam of purple light pulsed through the Bridge. 'The following fines have been added to your toll: crossing the Cos-Moat without permission, not using proper drawbridge protocol, and endangering local wildlife. State your name and your reasons for visiting Xion.'

Peri gulped. He could have kicked himself. He should have thought of a cover story. 'I . . . I . . .' he spluttered.

'Peace in space, Toll-Taker Xerallon,' Diesel said. 'We apologise for our rude behaviour. We're astro-nomads. We need extra fuel as well as repairs to our nav-system. My pilot is quite useless without a navigation computer telling him where to go. Last week, he almost flew us into a moon. We were lucky to crash into your lovely Cos-Moat.'

The screen was icing up, but Peri could see the Toll-Taker nod. 'Your ship's certainly a relic from a technology-stunted solar system. I'm surprised that junk can fly.'

Peri wanted to glare at the Toll-Taker. His ship wasn't junk. His parents had helped make the *Phoenix* better than anything in the universe. But arguing would only endanger the mission, so he kept quiet.

'Yes, you're right, of course,' Diesel told

the guard. 'It's almost embarrassing to fly – practically useless.'

Peri was impressed. Diesel was cool under pressure. It must have been his upbringing as the emperor's son – he knew exactly how to deal with the Toll-Taker.

'Access granted,' said the Toll-Taker. 'Please beam over payment.'

'Payment?' Peri whispered to Diesel. 'What are we . . . ?'

'Certainly, officer,' said Diesel, cutting Peri off. 'How would you like your payment?'

'Our scanners have already picked items of value.'

Peri held his breath, worried what the Xions wanted to take. White ice crystals had formed over the screen. When he scraped them away and saw the InfoBox, he almost laughed.

IDENTIFIED: plastic storage devices
and rich organic fertiliser.

'Peri,' Diesel whispered. 'What's "rich organic fertiliser"?'

'Erm . . .' Peri paused, 'I think they want plastic recycling bins and the contents of our space-toilets.'

Diesel's band of hair went limp and turned green. He cupped a hand over his mouth. 'You mean . . . They want our . . . ? Yuck!'

'Thank you, officer,' Peri told the Toll-Taker. 'Beam away.'

A light flashed to confirm the toll had been taken, and the barrier blocking the ramp on to the space highway vanished. On the com-screen Peri noticed another uniformed Toll-Taker rush into the booth. The official whispered something into the other Toll-Taker's ear. Both glared at the *Phoenix*.

This can't be good, thought Peri. He activated the main engines. 'Let's get out of here,' Peri shouted to Diesel as he roared the *Phoenix* down the nearest lane of the space highway.

Chapter 4

The silver-and-purple Astrophalt shimmered as the space highway twisted and stretched around the orange-and-blue planet below. If it wasn't for their mission to rescue the kidnapped prince, Peri could have raced along the shifting Astrophalt all day. It was just like playing a 3-D game, except, the web of ice crystals over the 360-monitor made it harder to see where he was going. The lane ahead looked clear, so Peri pulled the throttle to maximum.

'Next stop Xion!' he shouted as the *Phoenix* burst forward.

The intercom crackled into life with the sound of chattering teeth. 'Will you . . . space-monkeys . . . turn up the . . . hea-hea-heating' the Meigwor stuttered over the intercom. 'I'm f-f-f-f-free-eezing down here.'

Blue tears fell from Diesel's cheeks all over the gunnery station as he shook with laughter.

'Sorry, Otto,' Peri replied, trying to ignore Diesel. He spun the thermo-dial back and saw his Expedition Wear change colour again.

Outside, an asteroid-size super-neon sign pointed to a way-station. Behind the sign, an enormous transparent dome floated in the air. An instant translation appeared on screen.

'"Food! Souvenirs! Lizard wrestling!" I wish we had time to check *that* out,' Peri said.

Shhhhuurpt. The door to the Bridge opened as Otto shuffled in.

Diesel leaned over and whispered, 'Is it me or has he shrunk?'

Peri glanced over his shoulder. Otto's arms and neck did seem shorter.

'Cloak the ship!' Otto pushed Peri aside and stabbed at the control panel. A map of the space highway appeared on the monitor. 'Exit 1427-A7!'

Peri activated the cloak and navigated to the exit ramp. The Astrophalt ended abruptly above a pulsing blue vortex big enough only for a single vessel.

'Local transport vortex detected,' the ship announced. 'Hold tight.'

Before Peri could ask if they needed Superluminal speed the vortex spat the *Phoenix* out. They were hovering over a barren landscape. Small twisters of orange dust scoured the pockmarked ground. InfoBoxes popped up on the monitor, arrows scattered everywhere: *Collapsed CO_2 mine, toxic waterhole, mining-lice infestation.*

Peri stared at the swirling pools of putrid-green and snotty-brown liquid. 'No wonder they don't respect anyone else's planet. Look at those poisonous swamps.'

'Ignore them!' Otto said. 'Aim for the smog.'

Peri steered the *Phoenix* over a huge crater filled with machines spewing rocks into the air. He then headed for a skyline that appeared to be wrapped in smog. In the centre of the smoking chimneys and the block industrial buildings stood a sprawling marble palace.

'The Xion capital!' Otto said. 'Depressing, isn't it? The prince is in that palace. Head to that disused factory! We can land safely in there!'

Peri guided the *Phoenix* into the hollow shell of the building that Otto had pointed to. He was careful to avoid the metal struts holding up the crumbling brick walls. A single knock would bring the whole building down.

The rubble floor shifted under the ship's weight, but the landing gear automatically adjusted. Peri looked around and realised why Otto had chosen the spot. The walls surrounding the *Phoenix* would keep it hidden from alien eyes.

'Let's go!' Otto ordered. 'We've wasted enough time. Let's go get the prince.'

'Wait a second.' Peri studied the blinking lights of the atmospheric sensors. 'Diesel, adjust your oxy-modifiers to Carbon-4 Mode. Xion seems to be a carbon-rich planet.'

Peri pressed a nano-dial surgically implanted between his ribs. It beeped four times. His lungs twitched as if he needed to cough, then they expanded in his chest.

'What was that?!' Otto asked.

'Every IF cadet has a hydrogen bubble in their lungs,' Diesel replied, coughing as his lungs adjusted. 'The oxy-modifier allows us to breathe in any atmosphere in the universe.'

'Otherwise we'd suffocate outside in about seven seconds,' Peri added.

Otto shook his head in disbelief. 'You're so primitive!' he said. He lead them down the mauve-lit corridor into the air-lock. 'Come on, let's go.'

As they neared the end of the corridor, Peri noticed a small yellow button on the wall and stopped. He didn't know what it did, but his fingers tingled to press it. As he did, the ship announced, 'Planet name: Xion. Recommend: footwear adjustment for lighter gravity.'

Robotic arms shot out of the walls, lifting him and Diesel into the air. Two more arms appeared. They peeled the thick magnetic soles off Peri's space boots and clamped on new super-thin ones. The boots turned dusty orange.

'Camouflaged, too,' Peri said as the arms lowered him and Diesel.

Otto was shaking with laughter. 'I can't believe what you have to go through just to go outside!'

'At least we've created the technology to do it,' said Peri, bristling.

'Yes!' said Otto, holding his belly. 'But truly advanced species don't need such tricks!'

'What about you?' Peri asked. 'You think a Meigwor can walk around unnoticed?'

Otto tapped the lumps on his neck. 'Watch!'

He folded his long arms behind his back, so that they were now on opposite sides. His arms looked almost normal length. Otto yanked two rings from the side of his ammo-belts. A cloak sprang from around his shoulders, hiding the extra length of arms. He folded the collar up to cover his freakishly long, lumpy neck.

'Amazing!' Diesel exclaimed, sarcastically. 'I hadn't realised you Meigwors were such masters of disguise.'

Otto smiled. Peri shook his head and pressed the panel for the exit. The door swung open and hot sticky air blasted them. Peri and Diesel's Expedition Wear turned blue to cool them, but it was still hot. The ramp appeared and they followed Otto to the ground and through the disused factory.

As they walked the streets of Xion, Peri realised Otto's disguise worked. It wasn't a good disguise, but in the hazy light he went unnoticed. Luckily, the Xions appeared to look almost human but had webbed fingers and smelt of Saturnian squid.

Peri whispered to Otto, 'Why don't they have pincer claws and antennae like the Xions who beamed aboard our ship?'

'Shh,' Otto hissed back. 'The Xions wear special battle suits to scare their enemies! Now follow me and keep quiet!'

The enormous palace walls cast shadows over the many small shops selling everything from 'Organic fertiliser, fresh for eating!' to 'Live grubs jewellery!' Peri felt sick. The creamy maggots squirming along the necklaces looked revolting.

Thankfully, as they got closer to the palace, they left behind the traders cooking up foul brews, and the streets became deserted.

The palace walls were covered with cameras and laser wires. Peri and Diesel stopped. The palace gates were huge and made from twisted bits of ships, carefully moulded into decorative swirls. In among alien names, Peri noticed the names of ships from the IF fleet lost on deep-space missions:

IFSS *Blade*, IFSS *Grace*. Despite the humid heat, even his circuits felt cold with fear. If the Xions had defeated the pride of the IF fleet, what chance did he and Diesel have of avenging the Milky Way against such a terrible enemy?

'Is Otto mad?' Diesel asked. 'Does he think he can just walk in?'

Peri saw Otto marching up to the gates. There was a shout of 'Stop or Die'.

Out of the shadows beside the gates, four guards stepped out pointing assault blasters straight at them.

Oh no, thought Peri. *Otto's got us into deep cosmic-trouble.*

Chapter 5

Peri couldn't believe it. Otto kept walking even as the guards charged up their assault blasters. It was like Otto was offering himself up to a firing squad.

A guard raised a webbed hand to ward Otto back. 'Don't come any closer.'

'Stay behind Otto,' Diesel whispered to Peri. 'If they shoot, they'll hit him first.'

Otto stopped beside the nearest guard, who looked as surprised as Peri was. What was the Meigwor up to?

Otto pulled down his collar. Before the

guards could react, Otto uttered a low, guttural sound. His neck bulged and twisted. It was a bit like a giant Martian wildcat purring and it made the circuitry in Peri's head buzz.

Peri clamped his hands over his ears. It was a horrible noise. He wondered why Otto was doing it. But then he noticed that the guards had stopped moving. It was as

if Otto had turned them to stone. Peri couldn't believe his eyes.

Diesel prodded one of the guards. 'Cool, guard-cicles.'

'Stop messing around!' Otto unhooked a communication device from a guard's belt.

Peri expected some sort of explanation from the bounty hunter. Instead, Otto pushed the gates open and walked into a huge courtyard of polished orange marble. Peri looked at Diesel, but the gunner just shrugged and followed Otto. Peri ran after them both.

The courtyard was surrounded by a dozen buildings which dripped with gilding, statues and ornate decorations. Otto made for the most imposing of the palace buildings. Above the palace's massive wooden doors was the inscription: *Respect the King or DIE PAINFULLY*.

Otto pulled Peri and Diesel to the side of the door. The Meigwor peered inside. 'Listen, space-monkeys!' he said, turning to them. He was trying to whisper but his booming voice carried. 'Xions can't handle low-frequency noise! If we can break into their communications channels, we can frazzle their entire nervous system! Watch this!'

Peri and Diesel peeked around the door. A group of guards stood in the corridor. An officer was issuing orders. Otto raised the communications device to his neck and pressed a button to communicate on all channels. His neck throbbed again and a deep noise rumbled from his throat. The officer seized up in mid-speech, along with the other guards.

Peri felt an electric shiver run through him. 'You mean you've frozen everyone in the palace?'

'Of course, how else can we get our hands on . . . I mean, *rescue* the prince?!'

Peri smiled at the bounty hunter, but he felt a little uneasy about Otto's ability. If he could do that to Xions, what could he do to humans and Martians?

Otto led them through the ornately carved corridors. The walls and ceiling were covered in gold-leaf. Holograms of Xion battle victories lined the walls as well as empty suits of their fearsome black-shell battle armour. Peri couldn't help imagining the suit's bulging eye-slits watching them.

'Here we are!' Otto stopped them at an intersection. 'According to my sources, the prince may be locked in a cellar!'

What sources? Peri wondered, as Otto pulled off his cloak and unrolled his arms. He stomped up and down the orange-tiled corridor until he heard a hollow thud. He traced the tile with his finger and levered the trapdoor open. A rancid smell of damp and decay wafted up from the dark hole. It smelt worse than the farting swamps of Venus.

'You two go down and rescue him!' Otto ordered them.

'You're not in charge,' Diesel sneered. 'And he's *your* prince. Why don't *you* do it?'

Otto shook his head. 'I will search for the prince, too, but I must stay up here in case the guards unfreeze! I will fight the Xions!'

'Fine,' Diesel growled, seeing that Otto did have a point.

Peri followed the gunner down the slime-covered rusting metal rungs.

If only it was galactic glow-in-the-dark slime, thought Peri. *This cellar's darker than a black hole.*

Peri stepped off the ladder into some-thing very soft and sticky. 'Eeeew!'

That explains the smell, he thought. His space boots glowed for an instant as they automatically burnt away whatever he had stepped in. Expedition Wear rocked!

'Here, Prince, Prince, Prince,' Diesel called.

'He's royalty, not a cat,' Peri hissed.

'With the Meigwors, anything is possi-ble,' muttered Diesel, before bellowing, 'Your Royal Highness, you-hoo?'

Yooou-hoooo-hooo-hoo. The sound echoed through the cellar.

Peri stumbled forward in the dark. He couldn't even see if he was walking in a straight line. He bumped into something.

'Hey, lamizoid, watch it!' Diesel snapped.

'I'm not Martian. I can't see in the dark.'

There was an awkward silence. Something wasn't right. 'Wait a minute . . .' he muttered, staring through the blackness at where he thought Diesel was.

'Why aren't your eyes glowing?' he asked. 'Don't Martians have illumovision? Shouldn't you be able to see in the dark?'

'Um, well . . .' Diesel muttered. Peri couldn't see Diesel's face, but he could hear a squeak of embarrassment in the gunner's voice. 'Just because illumovision isn't part of my half-Martian blood, doesn't mean I'm not all Martian where it counts. I could beat you any day with both eyes shut and –'

'Hey, space-monkeys!' Otto bellowed. 'We can leave now! I've found the prince!'

Peri shook his head. *It figures. Otto sent us down here for nothing.*

Diesel didn't seem to mind. They stumbled through the darkness until they spotted the slimy rungs of the ladder. As

Peri climbed out, he found Otto wrestling with a large silver blanket. It thrashed about in his arms, mumbling and cursing.

'Otto,' Peri demanded. 'What on Neptune is going on?'

'Nothing!' Otto shouted. He prodded the blanket, threatening whatever, or whoever, was inside as he did. 'You can shut up, or I'll let the Earthlings blast you.'

Otto glanced at Peri and Diesel. 'It's for his own safety! He's been brainwashed by the evil Xions!' Otto's lipless mouth slid into a sheepish smile. 'Just a moment!'

Otto pulled a rope from a utility pouch and lassoed it around the blanket. The rope spun around the prince, tying the silver material into a bundle before vanishing. Otto flung the bundle over his shoulder. 'We go now!'

But Otto didn't even manage a single

step. *Eeeerrraaaa-eeerrraaa!* Alarms blasted from every direction. Metal gates crashed between the archways in the corridor, sealing them off from the rest of the palace.

Chapter 6

Eeeerrraaaa-eeerrrraaaa. The palace alarms were screeching at full volume.

One of the gates had jammed halfway down. Peri, Diesel and Otto ducked under it and ran.

They passed a picture of the Xion king in his full battle gear. Instead of black, his shell was a brilliant gold. He held the suit's helmet under his arm, but his hands were pincer claws and the suit's scorpion tail curled behind him. Peri couldn't help feeling their daring rescue was about to end badly.

Peri urged his crew on, turning this way then that, down the twisting corridors. It was getting so hot and stuffy that even the Expedition Wear struggled to keep them cool. They raced around the next corner and another portrait of the King of Xion greeted them. It was the same as the last one.

'Don't they have any other pictures of the king?' Diesel wondered aloud.

'Wait a minute,' said Peri, trying to catch his breath. 'We're running in circles.'

'Nonsense!' snapped Otto, adjusting the silver bundle over his shoulder. 'Meigwors have a keen sense of direction!'

'Listen,' Peri panted, supporting himself up against the corridor. 'We've seen this picture twice already.'

Otto licked the sweat off his forehead with his tongue. 'No, we haven't!'

'Yes, we have,' panted Diesel. 'It's a self-repeating maze.'

'We're trapped,' Peri said. Anger pulsed through him, as a computerised voice rang out inside his head:

Fight-or-Flight — activated.

That had never happened before. Peri's Expedition Wear tightened as his muscles swelled. His feet tingled and his arms throbbed. He didn't know what was happening. Peri's circuits buzzed with energy. His bionic abilities obviously extended beyond the *Phoenix*, but it was no time to test them! He didn't know what he'd activated, or how to switch it off.

'I'm going to get us out of here,' Peri told Otto and Diesel. His legs powered forward. Without hesitation, he grabbed hold of the metal bars that were blocking their way and twisted. *Snap!* Peri gasped at his super-human strength, but continued to pull bars from the gate as though they were nothing more than matchsticks. *Snap! Snap!*

Before either of the others could react, Peri heard the sound of the palace guards' heavy boots thundering along the marble corridors behind them. The effects of Otto's freezing trick must have worn off. Peri grabbed Diesel and Otto and pulled them through the gap in the gate.

'Run!' Peri sprinted down the marble corridor.

The corridor ahead was clear, so he put on an extra spurt of speed. As he reached the next junction his body stopped so suddenly he thought his eyes would pop out. One moment he had been zooming down the corridor, the next his muscles were fighting to keep him upright. His heart was pounding fast enough to explode. What if he had overdone it and snapped some internal wiring or tripped a switch?

He glanced behind him. Diesel and Otto were still struggling to catch up. The palace guards were in hot pursuit. He tried to move forward again, but his legs were frozen. Instead, he heard the calm computerised voice inside his head say: *Flesh-vaporising trap, calculating optimal route to avoid. Calculation done.*

Suddenly, he could see the red beams of the deadly rays criss-crossing the junction.

Ready in, three, two . . .

Peri could do nothing to stop his body crouching. He couldn't even close his eyes.

. . . one!

He leapt higher into the air than he had ever done outside of a 3-D game or zero-gravity training. He soared up, his hair brushing the ceiling. He felt so powerful and skilled. He tucked into a double somersault, tumbling perfectly through the gaps in the flesh-vaporising rays.

Not even Diesel could do that!

His body knew what to do next. Instantly, it twisted and launched him into a backflip, followed by a perfectly controlled forward roll. Peri landed in front of a control panel and his hand smashed into it. Sparks flew as a jolt of

energy burst from his arm into the wall. Smoke poured out between the cracks in the plaster and the beams criss-crossing the room flickered and faded away.

'All clear!' Peri shouted as he super-charged down the final corridor to the palace courtyard. *I could get used to being bionic,* he thought. But as he did, the floor slid away to reveal a pit lined with deadly spikes. He skidded to a stop a centimetre from the edge of the trap.

'The guards have powered up their lasers!' shouted Otto. He and Diesel were getting closer.

Zap-zap-zap-kaaapowww! Laser fire blasted the walls around him, raining down frag-ments of stone.

Otto sprinted ahead of Diesel. He squealed when he saw the pit for the first time. Peri grabbed the Meigwor by his ammo-belts and threw him and the prince clean across.

Zap-zap-zap-sssizz. The laser fire was getting closer.

'Come on, Diesel,' Peri urged.

'I'm coming!' The gunner put on an extra burst and raced towards Peri. When he saw the pit, his eyes widened and his band of hair turned plasma-white.

'Don't stop, keep going!' Peri called. 'I'm going to catapult you across!'

'Are you crazy?' yelled Diesel.

'Just trust me!' Peri grabbed Diesel and tossed him over the deadly spikes.

Peri took one last look at the approaching guards, glanced across the pit and hoped his bionic body wouldn't let him down. He prepared himself to take a running leap.

Zap-zap-boom!

The ceiling began to crumble and rain down around him. He had to go now. He fixed his eyes on Diesel and went for it. As he jumped, it felt as though he was leaving his stomach behind. He couldn't help but imagine falling on to the spikes.

But he made it. He rolled as he landed and then stood up. *Phew!*

Zap-zap-fhizzz. A laser blast punched against his shoulder, knocking him down. Peri was ready for burning pain to rip through his circuits, but nothing happened. He pressed his hand against his shoulder, but found only a small hole burnt into his jacket. *I'm bionic* and *lucky!*

As he crawled towards Otto and Diesel, his suit began to buzz, changing colour from blue to the same dusty orange as the marble in the palace. The suit's material began to harden. Peri stood up. Another

laser blast hit him, but this time it ricocheted off, almost hitting Otto.

'Diesel!' Peri exclaimed. 'Our suits are
laser-proof!'

'You two hold back the guards, then!' Otto
shouted. 'I must get the prince to safety!'

They broke out into the palace courtyard. Peri glanced behind. Not a single
guard had pursued them over the spiked
pit. They had escaped! He punched the air.
All they needed to do now was make it to
the *Phoenix*, return to Meigwor and get
Selene back.

'Let's go,' Peri urged, but as he took
another step, his legs buckled. He only just
stopped himself from falling. Something
was wrong. His bionic body was feeling
sooo heavy, but why? He tried to force
himself on, but the air was thickening
around him. 'Activate Fight-or-Flight,' he

muttered desperately, but his body slowed. *Some robot I am,* he thought. *I don't even know how to operate myself.*

'Come on, Peri,' Diesel said. 'We've got to get out of here.'

Peri stumbled forward. Diesel grabbed him, stopping him from collapsing completely. Peri looked around. There wasn't a single guard in the courtyard.

'I can't believe it,' he said to Diesel, 'we got away with it.'

Diesel shook his head and pointed at the sky.

Peri looked up. 'Oh . . .'

Hundreds of Xion guards on cruisers were circling above the courtyard like a swarm of Neptunian Gnats. Every single one of them had their blasters aimed at Peri and his companions.

Chapter 7

The Xion cruisers looked like they meant serious, deadly business. Running was impossible. The cruisers were light and sleek, which meant they would also be fast and easy to manoeuvre through the narrow streets. The Xion guards had laser assault-blasters pressed against their shoulders, their webbed fingers poised to shoot. They had bubble-like headphones protecting each ear from Otto's booming, hypnotic voice.

'Raise your hands, space-monkeys!' hissed

Otto. 'Before they take it as an excuse to kill first and ask questions later!'

'But why *haven't* they attacked?' Peri asked, lifting his arms.

'They probably want a public execution,' Diesel said, doing the same. 'Emperor Elliotte the First used to do that.'

'Shh,' Otto said. 'They might not know we have the prince! They could think we're just intruders!'

'Are you insane?' Peri said. 'Isn't it obvious we have him? What else do they think you have over your shoulder?'

'The blanket's invisible to them!' Otto whispered in a low voice, but it still felt as if he was shouting. 'Their eyes can't see certain types of silver! It's the wrong light-wavelength!'

'Is that why your blaster is silver?' Diesel asked.

'Exactly!' Otto grunted.

Peri couldn't see how that would help them. His arms were shaking from holding them in the air. It wouldn't be long before his whole body collapsed.

Out of the corner of his eye, Peri saw Otto slowly reaching for his weapon.

He's insane, thought Peri. *We're 700 per cent outgunned and in eighty times more trouble than we've ever been and he's still going for his blaster!*

'You're going to get us killed,' Peri hissed.

As Otto's hand reached his blaster's grip, angry red dots spread across his skin like the Ich'stein Pox. The red dots covered every bit of him, including his ammo-belts and his cloak.

'Don't move, Otto!' Diesel hissed. 'They have their laser sights on you.'

Otto raised his hand slowly away from

his blaster. He flicked a look at Peri. 'You'd
better follow the same advice!'

Peri glanced down at himself, then over
at Diesel. Otto was right. Red laser spots
danced over their bodies too.

A cruiser with a red stripe along its sleek
black sides hovered closer. The guard
sitting on it stood up. There was a large
badge on his chest and a row of medals. A
strange plume of feathers had been stuck

to the back of his helmet.

'Return the prince or perish,' he ordered. His voice was amplified by the loudspeakers in the courtyard. 'You have ten seconds to tell me what you have done with His Royal Excellency.'

'Ten . . .'

Peri glanced at the silver bundle on Otto's shoulder. If they handed over the prince, he was sure they'd be killed anyway for helping the Meigwors. It was odd that the Xions had called their enemy His Royal Excellency. Peri wouldn't have called Diesel by his official title in a million light years.

It's probably a Xion trick to confuse us, he thought.

'Nine . . .'

There's only one thing for it.

'Eight . . .'

'We can't let them take the prince,' Peri

whispered to Diesel. 'Even if we die trying to defend him.'

'But he's Meigwor,' Diesel replied.

'It doesn't matter,' Peri said. 'We've got to do our duty and protect him!'

'Seven . . .'

'If we fail to return the Prince,' Peri said, 'we'll never see Selene again.'

'Four . . . Three . . .'

'Come and get us, you Xion cowards!' Otto boomed.

'Two . . .'

Otto threw his head back and roared: 'You couldn't pulverise a space-bug with a planet-buster!'

'One . . .'

Peri couldn't let these aliens win. He had to do something to stop them.

'Ready!' screamed the Xion commander. 'Aim!'

But what could he do? He was unarmed, trapped – helpless.

'Fire!' barked the commander.

Hundreds of searing red beams of lasers burst from the assault-blasters.

Peri felt his hands thrusting forward. 'Noooo!' he screamed.

A brilliant flash of electric blue light erupted from his outstretched fingers. The air crackled with energy as the laser beams were vaporised midair.

Peri stared at his hands in amazement. 'What in the Milky Way was that?' he gasped.

'There's only one thing that disrupts laser beams – an electromagnetic pulse!' Otto exclaimed.

'Yeah, well done, Peri,' Diesel muttered moodily. 'But *I'm* the gunner. Next time you find a cool gadget on the *Phoenix*, tell me before you take it or there'll be trouble.'

'Yeah,' said Peri, hiding his hands behind his back. Diesel had no idea Peri was part-bionic. 'I'll do that next time.'

Some of the Xion guards examined their weapons; others beat theirs against the side of their cruisers to see if they could make them work again.

'We must get out of here fast,' said Peri but, as he tried to step forward, his vision swam as though he was back in the Cos-Moat. 'Activate engines,' he mumbled.

'It must be heatstroke,' Diesel said. 'You're not making sense, Peri.'

It was no good. Peri's legs buckled under him and he fell to the ground. His body refused to respond to his commands. He was utterly spent.

This is the end for me, he thought.

Diesel knelt beside him, trying to loosen Peri's Expedition Wear jacket.

Peri looked up. A Xion cruiser had broken formation and was speeding towards them. It took him a moment to realise the guard had tossed aside his useless state-of-the-art weapon and was reaching for an old-fashioned machine-blaster. Peri tried to warn the others, but all he could speak was gibberish, 'Guuaaaa-guaaaarr-aarrd.'

The voice in his head was repeating a warning:

Bionic batteries drained. Bionic batteries drained.

The electromagnetic blast must have taken the last of his energy. After all they had been through to rescue the prince, had he blown the entire mission because he didn't know how to operate his own body?

'Leave without me,' Peri said. 'I don't have the energy to stand, let alone run.'

'I'm not leaving you,' said Diesel. 'You're not getting away from me and Otto that easily . . .'

'Get the prince back to the *Phoenix*. We can't fail on our mission,' Peri ordered. 'I'll fight them off as long as I can.'

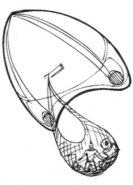

Chapter 8

Otto ripped a smoke grenade from his ammunition belts. He whipped the pin out with his tongue and threw it towards the guards. The grenade exploded in a cloud of lurid yellow smoke.

'Quick, before the smokescreen disappears!' Otto snapped, grabbing Diesel and trying to pull him away from Peri, but the half-Martian gunner wouldn't budge.

'We're not leaving Peri!' Diesel shouted, trying to shake off the Meigwor. But Otto was already dragging him towards the palace gatehouse. 'This isn't the end!' Diesel shouted over his shoulder. 'Keep fighting, Peri!'

'Catch!' Otto shouted from the shadow of the gatehouse. The Meigwor threw him a couple of smoke grenades, but they fell short and rattled against the marble, out of Peri's reach.

Otto vanished out of the palace gates, dragging Diesel behind him.

As Peri reached out for the grenades,

sharp chips of marble stung his arms as blaster rounds ricocheted off the ground. There was a stone bench close by. Peri used all his strength to crawl towards the shelter.

I wish the Phoenix *was here,* he thought.

He wouldn't be able to hold off the palace guard for much longer. *At least I helped Otto and Diesel make a clean getaway. They'll get Selene back. The mission will be a success.*

Peri glanced over the bench and saw a swarm of palace cruisers searching the city for Otto and Diesel. In the distance the sleek egg shape of the *Phoenix* rose like a white sun over the city. The guard cruisers would be no match against his ship.

But no one's on board, he realised. *Otto and Diesel couldn't have made it back that quickly.*

Peri's stomach twisted like a hatching space-eel. 'Someone's stealing my ship!'

More blaster rounds exploded against the

bench, showering Peri with splinters of orange marble, forcing him to duck. He couldn't believe it. Everything was lost. The prince was about to be recaptured and he was about to face his final fight. It wasn't fair.

Then the guards stopped firing and Peri peered over the bench. He saw the guards getting off their cruisers and walking towards him with laser blasters held ready.

Something roared overhead. Peri expected to see another Xion ship. But it was the *Phoenix*! It had come to save him!

The *Phoenix* fired at the palace guards, forcing them to retreat. As the Xions ran for cover, an electro-laser net whipped down from the ship. It caught Peri and lifted him up. Diesel, Otto and the foil-wrapped prince were already hanging there.

'We need to get inside the ship, Diesel!' Peri shouted as the Xion guards opened

fire again from the courtyard below. 'We're sitting ducks in this net!'

'Great plan,' Diesel called back. 'Why didn't I think of that? Oh, yes — because there's no way in!'

If the ship had listened to Peri's commands once, it could do it again! 'Evasive manoeuvres,' he shouted, hoping the *Phoenix* would understand.

'You've finally gone cos-mad, Peri,' muttered Diesel. 'I told you, we can't get back inside the —'

But before Diesel could say another word, the *Phoenix* shot off. Peri was thrown against his gunner as the net skimmed the rooftops. The ship stayed low over the city to stop the cruisers attacking from below and prevent the heavier gunships from firing down on them. The net swung from side to side, narrowly missing jagged turrets and smoking chimneys.

The *Phoenix* burst out of the city — heading straight for a floating minefield. Peri had never felt so terrified as the spaceship turned and twisted, dodging the huge spiked mines hovering like birds of prey. Deep down he knew he had to trust the ship. As soon as it cleared the minefield, it slowed down. Diesel pushed Peri away.

'I wasn't scared, you know,' Diesel muttered.

Peri sighed, but it was good to have things back to normal. Above him, a hatch opened and the electro-laser net started retracting back into the ship.

Maybe they were going to make it after all.

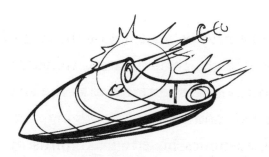

Chapter 9

The electro-laser net dropped them on to the Bridge and vanished. The 360-monitor pulsed into life, showing the desert wastelands they were flying over. There was not a Xion vessel in sight.

The ship's robotic voice sounded through the speakers: '*Autopilot disengaged. Cloaking device activated.*'

Every muscle in Peri's body felt sore. Every wire and circuit felt burnt out. A low hum pulsed in his head accompanied by a short beep to warn him to recharge. It would have to wait. Diesel helped him to the captain's chair then positioned himself at the gunner's station and began reviewing their weapons status.

There was a *shruupt* behind him. Peri glanced round to see Otto vanish through the door with the prince. 'Oh, great. Just when we need him, he disappears. How are we supposed to know how to get off this planet?'

Diesel coughed. 'Leave the plan to me. I can get us back into space.'

Diesel pulled up a 3-D map of the space highway.

'We can't go back by the Toll-Takers. I don't think we can fool them twice. And even if we could, the Xion guards have probably issued a big "WANTED" poster with our pictures on it.'

'Why would we need to go back through the Toll-Takers?' Diesel asked.

'I don't suppose you remember the Cos-Moat and the space-sharks?'

'That was coming in!' said Diesel smugly. 'If we use Superluminal speed, we could just burst straight through the Cos-Moat. There's no risk of crashing into a planet on the other side.'

'I'll check the energy gauges.' Peri's hand darted over the control panel. The *Phoenix* had just enough power to activate Superluminal speed, but not enough for them to navigate it accurately. 'If we survive, we could end up anywhere.'

'Do you have a better idea?' Diesel asked.

Peri looked at the damage reports. The ship was in bad shape after its tangle with the palace guards. 'No, I don't,' he said. 'Let's go for it — Superluminal, right through the Cos-Moat.'

The astro-harness strapped him in.

Something warm tingled up his back. It wasn't frightening, but refreshing. A trickle of power was flowing from the chair into his body, giving him the extra energy he needed.

A small monitor appeared from the chair's armrest and flashed into life.

'Looks like we've got trouble, Diesel,' Peri said. 'The *Phoenix* has detected Xion ships heading our way.'

Peri powered up the *Phoenix* and set a course for the space highway. The ship shook as it tore through the atmosphere into space.

Peri dodged around yet another mine-field of micro-clusters before ducking between the vast, shifting tangle of Astrophalt. They swooped across a dozen-lane mega highway and swung down towards a vortex slipway, narrowly avoiding being sucked back down to the planet. They burst free of the space highway and hurtled towards the Cos-Moat.

'Prepare for Superluminal speed!' Peri shouted into the intercom. They had to engage the engines before hitting the corrosive gloop.

With a touch of his hand, the smooth red Superluminal speed panel slid open to reveal two switches. He flicked them and braced himself, but nothing happened.

The display flashed up: *More Power Needed*.

'Diesel, cut power to everything!'

Peri and Diesel shut down everything except the Superluminal engines and the shields. The 360-monitor and the Bridge lights flickered out. The display flashed green. The Superluminal engines were a go!

The ship rumbled as though there was a

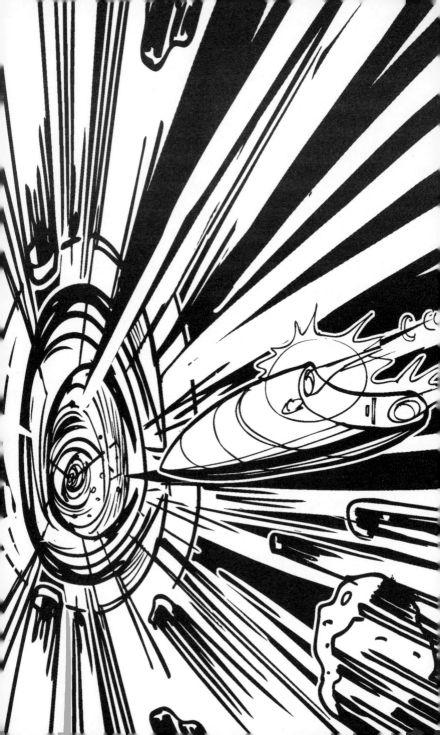

spacequake. The *Phoenix* shot forward, then slowed as it hit the gooey Cos-Moat.

'Come on!' urged Peri. 'You can do it!'

Like an elastic band snapping, the *Phoenix* pinged free and was catapulted across the galaxy at a speed faster than light. In complete darkness, Peri listened to the engines as their high-pitched whine trembled through the ship. It began to drop down, lower and lower, until the sound of the engine vanished.

Peri blinked as the Bridge lights came back on and the 360-monitor flashed to life. He activated the deep-space scanners for hostiles and dangers, but even *The Space Spotter's Guide* found nothing to report. They were in the middle of nowhere, just floating in empty space.

Solar-tastic, thought Peri, *a bit of peace in space for us!*

His back tingled as the chair started boosting his energy levels again. As Peri stood up, he noticed a flashing light on the message panel.

'Diesel, we've got a message. It's using IF code-encryptions.'

'Do you think it's from Earth?'

'We'd better find out before Otto returns.'

Peri pressed the button to play the message. A com-screen rose from the control panel and the message began to play. It was Selene! Her eyes were wide with panic. Her voice was barely above a whisper. She was obviously scared of something.

'Peri, Diesel, I — *crrrk, crrrk* — listen — *crrrk* . . . be careful — *crrrk* — the Meigwors are not what they seem. They were lying about . . .'

A blaster appeared in the screen and was pressed against Selene's temple. The image

on screen faded to white noise. The trans-mission was cut.

'Selene!' exclaimed Peri.

As the screen retracted into the console, Peri felt something sink inside of him. All the niggling doubts he had about Otto and the Meigwors could no longer be ignored.

'Diesel, we need to talk,' said Peri. *Shruupt.* The doors to the Bridge opened as he was speaking and Otto strolled in. Peri closed his mouth. The lumps on Otto's neck were throbbing in time with the strange whistling noise from the back of his throat.

'Talk about what?!' asked Otto. 'Talk about our successful mission? When we return to my planet, I will be honoured with a special parade and endless riches.'

Peri stared at the message console. Someone had been threatening Selene. He needed time to think.

'That's what we need to talk about,' replied Peri. 'We can't return to Meigwor straight away.'

The black patches around Otto's eyes darkened and spread across his crimson face. The lumps protruding from his neck twitched. 'What?!'

'We don't know where we are. The ship's sustained great damage. It needs repairing. Most of all . . . I'm exhausted. The ship doesn't fly without me as pilot.'

'I suppose we have no choice!' Otto said slowly. 'It's a shame! Your companion, Selene, must be missing you terribly!'

Peri turned to the *Phoenix*'s controls to hide his anger. How could Otto lie to his face?

But what were the Meigwors lying about? Whatever it was, Selene was in real danger.

Don't worry, Selene, he thought. *We're coming for you!*

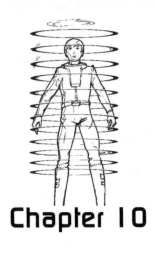

Chapter 10

Otto stomped towards the controls. His tongue flicked out, and narrowly missed Peri's nose. 'Show me these damage reports!' he said.

'Sure,' Peri said, changing the display on the 360-monitor.

As Otto studied the reports, Diesel spoke. 'Can I meet your prince? I'm sure he'd want to thank me. I did rescue him, after all.'

Otto spun around and glared at the gunner. 'Not on my life, half-Earthling!' he snapped. 'I must send a message to my general and tell him about your incompetence!'

'*Our* incompetence?' shouted Diesel. 'I think you'll find *we're* the ones who saved *your* stupid long neck.'

Otto flicked his black tongue across his lipless mouth like a lizard.

'Come on, Diesel,' Peri said, 'help me to the Med Centre.' The last thing he needed was another fight breaking out between Otto and Diesel. He needed time to think and talk to his gunner without the Meigwor around. 'Give Otto the Bridge so he can send his message.'

Diesel nodded, but he couldn't take his eyes off Otto. 'Don't make yourself too comfortable.'

Peri let Diesel support him to the nearest portal. All he had to do was think of the Med Centre and when the portal hissed open, there it was. In the centre of the room, a medical table lay waiting. Around it the latest medical technology clicked and whirled.

As the portal closed, Diesel coughed nervously and Peri glanced at him.

'There's something I need to tell you, Diesel,' Peri said.

'You're not human, are you?' Diesel said bluntly. 'After what happened on Xion, you can't deny it. You have super-strength. You can send out a pulse that stops laser fire – I checked the inventory, we don't have a gadget that does that. So what are you?'

Peri stared at his gunner, trying to decide whether he could trust him with the truth. Diesel was not fully human, either. He was half-Martian, and the son of an emperor. In a way, he was as different as Peri.

Peri glanced at the portal. Otto wouldn't

be able to hear them here. 'My full name is Experiment. I'm part-bionic. I was modified by my parents to operate the *Phoenix*. I think being on the ship flipped some sort of bionic switch inside me.'

Diesel's eyes opened wide. 'No kidding? You're part of the ship! I always thought there was something weird about you.'

'But you mustn't tell anyone,' Peri warned. 'If the Meigwors find out, they'll never let us go. I've got to fully recharge and then we've got to find out what Otto's really up to.'

Peri scanned all the buttons and dials in the Med Centre. He closed his eyes and stretched out one hand. He needed to concentrate on what the ship wanted him to do. He started to walk, being pulled like metal to a magnet. His fingers tingled. He opened his eyes and punched the glowing button beneath his hand.

The Med Centre went dark and thousands of thin blue lines of light scanned Peri from every angle. The lights flashed on and a deep blue pulse shot from the button he pressed and zapped him right between the eyes. He heard the computer voice inside his head: *Energy low. Specimen is self-charging. For more energy, eat fruits and vegetables and sleep.*

Peri was a bit disappointed. He'd hoped for something more high-tech, but he'd been programmed by his parents, who were always trying to get him to eat healthily.

Diesel took a step back and looked Peri up and down. 'So . . .'

'I'll be fine,' Peri said, with a shrug. 'We've got bigger things to deal with.'

Peri found a com panel in among the Medi-lasers and internal probes. He touched the screen and whispered, 'Computer, show us the location of everyone on board.'

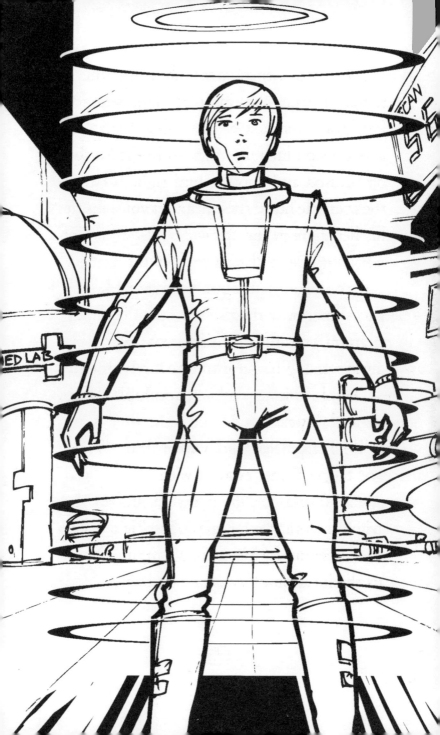

The screen blinked as it pulled up a map of the *Phoenix*. Four flashing lights appeared.

'Those two must be us,' Peri told Diesel, pointing at each in turn. 'This must be Otto, and this . . . is the prince.'

Diesel twitched his head from side to side. 'Where is he?'

Peri enlarged the image on the screen. 'Otto's sleeping quarters. Come on.'

He imagined themselves outside Otto's quarters and approached the portal.

Hiiissssss. The portal opened exactly opposite Otto's sleeping chamber. Peri glanced around to make sure they were alone. He placed his hand on the scanner beside the door. A bar of blue light moved down the panel. It turned red. Sparks erupted from Peri's fingers. The light flickered and turned green. The door to Otto's room slid open.

'Neat trick,' Diesel exclaimed. 'Wish *I* was part-bionic!'

They stepped inside. Peri gasped when he saw the prince chained to Otto's upright sleeping station and still wrapped in the silver blanket.

'This doesn't make any sense,' he muttered. 'Why would Otto treat a Meigwor prince like this?'

'You heard Selene,' Diesel said. 'He's been lying to us.' He tried to melt the chains with his laser blaster. He shook his head. 'It's no use. It's some sort of special Meigwor metal-alloy. I can't cut through it.'

Diesel stood on a chair and yanked the silver blanket from around the prisoner. The prince's neck was not freakishly long or lumpy. His skin was not red, and he had no dark patches around his eyes. In fact, he looked almost human except for his webbed fingers and a strong squid-like smell.

'He's not from Meigwor,' Peri said, feeling a numbness flow through him. 'He's from Xion!'

The prisoner's eyes bulged at the sight of Diesel and Peri. He spat out the gag stuffed in his mouth. 'I demand you let me go,' raged the prisoner. 'I am Prince Onix, first-born son and heir to the throne of Xion!

Unchain me or your deaths will be even more excruciatingly painful than they will be for this treason.'

'I don't understand,' Diesel whispered, ignoring the prisoner. 'Did Otto rescue the wrong person?'

Peri wished it was true, but he knew deep down it wasn't. Otto had been too pleased with himself. 'I think this was General Rouwgim and Otto's plan all along. The Meigwors, wanted to kidnap the Xion prince and they duped us into helping them!'

'Don't for an instant think that Xion will be held hostage by Meigwor any longer!' bellowed the prince. 'They won't get another drop of fuel in ransom!'

Peri shook his head. 'What you mean "be held hostage by Meigwor"?'

'Insolence! Don't talk to me unless I tell you to!' shouted the Prince. 'Everyone knows the Meigwors are the greatest inter-galactic bullies! Well, this is the last straw. My father, the king, will make sure that this debt is paid in the green-blood of the Meigwors. And, you, the stupid subspecies of humans, you will be treated harshly for aiding those galactic criminals! And, another thing, *huuumphh, aaagrahh!*'

The prince couldn't say anything more, because Diesel had stuffed the gag back into his mouth.

'Diesel!' Peri objected.

'What else am I supposed to do? *Listen* to him?'

Peri shrugged. He couldn't argue with that. 'Sorry, Your Highness,' Peri said to Prince Onix, giving a little bow. 'We'll think of something. We won't let Otto get away with tricking us into cosmic kidnapping.'

Peri turned to Diesel. 'Help me cover

him up and let's get out of here. We'd better go to the Med Centre in case Otto gets curious.'

Diesel nodded. The prince squirmed and protested, but Peri and Diesel finally covered him just like they had found him. Peri sealed the door to Otto's quarters.

As they stepped through the portal back to the Med Centre, Diesel asked, 'Who's really our enemy – the Xions or the Meigwors?'

'They both are. We've landed in the middle of a galactic war,' Peri said. 'And both sides are as bad as each other. The Meigwors are holding Selene hostage. The Xions have attacked Earth! There's only one side to be on now – our own!'

'So what's the plan, Peri?'

'I'm tired of being pushed around. It's about time we did what was right for *us*,' Peri replied. 'We've got to rescue Selene, then get out of this galactic conflict without the whole thing going supernova!'

Peri realised this was going to be their most difficult mission yet.

Will Peri and Diesel make it back to
Meigwor to rescue Selene?

Can they outsmart the double-crossing
Otto?

Find out! In . . .

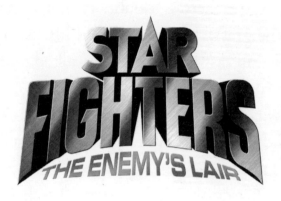

STAR
FIGHTERS
THE ENEMY'S LAIR

Turn over to read Chapter 1

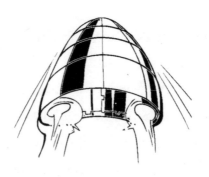

Chapter 1

'That treacherous double-crossing snake in the grass!' Diesel slammed his fist into the wall as he and Peri walked along the corridor that led to the Bridge of the *Phoenix*.

'I don't think they have grass on Meigwor,' Peri said.

'What do they have?' asked Diesel.

Peri shrugged. 'Trees, mostly. It's a jungle planet.'

'Snake in the trees, then. Let's push Otto into the air-lock and out into space and let the space-sharks chew on his big, long, rubbery neck!'

The strip of hair on Diesel's head was bristling like a Betelgeusian Pinfish's spines, and glowing bright orange, as it always did when the half-Martian was really angry.

They had just survived a dangerous mission on the planet Xion, supposedly to rescue a kidnapped Meigwor prince. The Meigwor had sent Otto, a bounty hunter, to lead the mission, but he had lied to Diesel and Peri. They had raided the Xion palace and captured someone, but it wasn't a *Meigwor* prince.

They hadn't rescued anyone – they had in fact *kidnapped* a Xion prince!

'Let's give him what he deserves –' Diesel said.

Peri held up his hand. 'If we throw Otto

to the space-sharks, the Meigwor will take it out on Selene.' Their friend was being held on Otto's home planet. 'It's time we stopped letting Otto boss us around. We need to rescue Selene and then return Prince Onix to Xion.'

'Otto won't back down without a fight.'

'Then we'll give him a fight!' Peri said. 'There are two of us — we should be able to disarm Otto and take back our ship.'

They were nearly at the Bridge now. Peri touched a button on the belt of his Expedition Wear. Diesel did the same. The surfaces of their suits became hard and shiny, like armour. Steel gauntlets emerged from the sleeves and covered their hands. Plexiglas helmets rose from the necks of the suits, encasing their heads in identical transparent, armoured bubbles.

'We might need more protection,' Peri said.

He touched the wall and a section slid smoothly back to reveal a chamber filled with vaporisers, blasters, phasers and jellifiers in countless different shapes and sizes.

'Look,' Peri said. 'Otto's been here.' He pointed to a silver flask on a shelf. It was the flask in which Otto kept his favourite drink, Meigwor Mudcreeper's Blood. Peri grimaced. 'Dunno how he can drink that stuff.'

Diesel picked up a little black weapon, with a wide, square muzzle. 'I've seen these in the training manual,' Diesel said. 'It's a duster.'

Diesel took aim at Otto's flask. He pressed the trigger. The flask dissolved into a small heap of fine grey dust.

'Wow,' Peri said. 'Better not use that unless it's life or death.'